The Legend of the Three Trees

THE LEGEND OF THE THREE TREES
from the screenplay by George Taweel and Rob Loos
is based on the traditional folk tale.

Copyright © 2001 by Tommy Nelson®, a division of Thomas Nelson, Inc.
Book adaptation by Catherine McCafferty.
Illustrations by Gene 'n Geppy Productions.

Published in Nashville, Tennessee, by Tommy Nelson®,
a division of Thomas Nelson, Inc.

Library of Congress Cataloging-in-Publication Data

McCafferty, Catherine.
    The legend of the three trees / by Catherine McCafferty.
      p. cm.
    Summary: An olive tree, an oak tree, and a pine tree dream of great
things, and their dreams are fulfilled when each fills an important role in
the life of Jesus.
    ISBN 0-8499-7595-6
    [1. Trees—Fiction. 2. Jesus Christ—Fiction.] I. Title.

PZ7.M122817 Le 2000
[E]—dc21
                                            00-050015

Printed in Singapore

06 07 08 09 10 TWP 17 16 15 14 13

The Legend of the

Three Trees

From the screenplay by
George Taweel and Rob Loos,
based on the traditional folk tale

Book adaptation by **Catherine McCafferty**

Illustrations by **Gene 'n Geppy Productions**

Thomas Nelson, Inc.
Nashville

Life burst into the world on the third day of Creation. From under the water, God brought forth the earth. Peeking up through the earth's soil, green plants waved like millions of tiny flags. Grasses, bushes, and trees grew into every size and shape.

The trees towered above all.
There were pine trees and poplar,
olive and oak, willow and walnut.
Each held its own seeds and fruits.

Their seeds and fruits scattered as animals carried them from the trees. In a green valley, a fox dropped an olive pit.

And along a rocky shore, a stork split open an acorn.

On a tall mountain, a goat accidentally
shook loose a seed from a pine cone.

The pit, the acorn, and the seed grew into saplings. Watered by the rain and warmed by the sun, they reached upward.

In time, a beautiful olive tree blossomed in the valley. A mighty oak stood on a rocky coast. And a tall pine tree stood on the mountain.

As each tree grew, it dreamed of what it would become.

The olive tree dreamed of becoming a beautiful and important treasure chest. Decorated with sparkling jewels, it would hold the greatest treasure in the world.

One day, when a woodsman came to the forest, it seemed that the olive tree's dream would come true.

The woodsman chose the olive tree from all the other trees. The olive tree trembled with happiness. At last, it would become a beautiful treasure chest!

The woodsman took the
olive tree to his workshop.
He cut the wood into
boards and hammered
them into a box shape.

But to the tree's surprise, the woodsman did not make
the box into a treasure chest. He did not polish the olive
tree's fine wood or fill the box with gold. Instead,
he dragged the box into a stable with messy
sheep, smelly cows, and noisy chickens.
The woodsman filled the box with hay.

The olive tree saw that it had become a manger, a mere feeding box for animals! It knew then that it would never hold a treasure.

As the olive tree's dream faded in the dusty stable, the oak tree looked out over the water with a dream of its own. Strong and proud, it dreamed that its mighty trunk would be made into a mighty ship that would carry a king!

One day, shipbuilders cut down the oak tree and hauled it to their boatyard. They sawed the broad trunk into boards. They bent the boards to form the sides of the boat.

With each passing day, the oak tree felt certain that its dream was coming true.

But when the shipbuilders were done, the oak felt small and weak. It had not become a mighty ship at all. Instead, it was a little fishing boat, launched on a calm lake. The mighty oak knew then that a king would never sail in a little fishing boat.

High on the mountainside above the oak boat, the pine tree stood tall. Many times, it saw people in the valley looking up. The pine tree hoped that its towering branches would remind people of the glory of God's Creation. It dreamed that it would always stay on the mountain and point people to God.

One night, a fierce storm shook the mountain. The pine tree bent and swayed in the powerful wind. As thunder boomed, a bolt of lightning flashed from the sky and splintered the tree's trunk.

With a sound almost as loud
as the thunder, the pine tree
crashed to the ground.

The pine tree's dream crashed down with it. No one would ever look up to it again. Its long trunk now just blocked the mountain road. The tree thought that things could not possibly get worse. But then strong soldiers hauled it to a scrapyard.

Unused and forgotten, the pine lay on a heap of old lumber. It knew then that a piece of scrap wood could never point people to God.

Many years passed. The trees' great dreams seemed
so far away that they stopped thinking about them.

For what greatness could come to a feed box, a fishing boat, and scrap wood?

But God had His own plan for each of the trees.

One night, shepherds keeping watch over their flock saw an angel. A great light shone all around. The angel told them not to be afraid, for their Savior had been born in Bethlehem. Just as the angel had said, the shepherds found the baby lying in a manger.

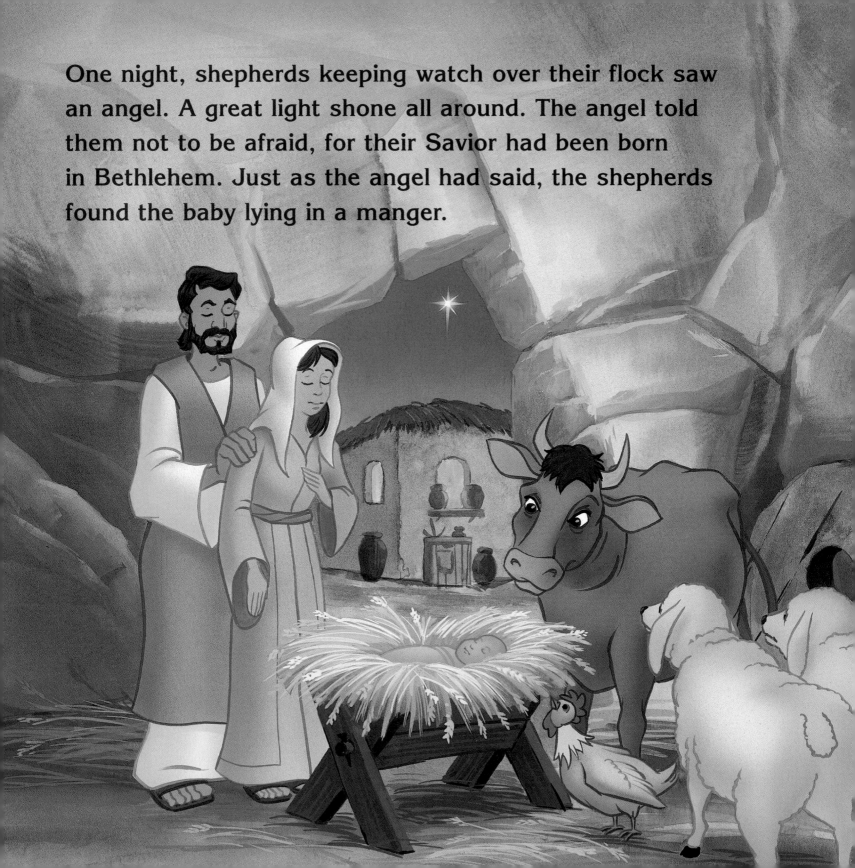

The olive tree had not become a treasure chest, but now, as a manger, it held the greatest treasure of all time—God's only Son, Jesus.

The infant Jesus grew into a man, and the man traveled to the very lake that held the oak fishing boat. One day, the little boat carried Jesus onto the lake with the fishermen. Suddenly, a great storm swept over the lake. Water washed into the boat. The oak boat struggled with all of its strength so it would not sink.

"Quiet! Be still,"
Jesus said. The storm
stopped. The oak boat felt Jesus'
power. The boat had never carried a king
of this world. But now it carried the King of Kings!

The pine tree knew nothing of Jesus or His miracles. But one morning, it heard angry voices in the distance. "Crucify him!" the people yelled. Soldiers came to the scrapyard and grabbed the forgotten pine. The pine tree expected to be cut into firewood. Instead, the soldiers cut its trunk into two pieces to make a cross.

Then they laid the cross on Jesus' back.

On a hillside, under a blackening sky, the pine cross swayed as the soldiers raised it. It did not know whether it could bear the weight of the man upon it. The pine tree had wanted only to point people to God. Now, it knew, it would become a sign of death.

Jesus died that day to take away the sins of all who believe in Him. He was taken down from the cross and laid inside a tomb. Then a wondrous thing happened. Three days later, Jesus rose to life again. And so Jesus fulfilled His heavenly Father's plan for Him.

And what of the three trees? They, too, had fulfilled God's plans for them. Miraculously, God's plans had taken them beyond their youthful dreams.

The olive-wood manger had held the greatest treasure of all, God's beloved only Son.

The oak fishing boat had carried the King of Kings, God's Son, during His work on earth.

And to this day, the cross points people to God as a symbol of His great love for us.

Sometimes, the dreams that we have for ourselves are much smaller than the dreams that God has for us. The three trees' dreams came true, just not in the way they imagined. And so it is with each of us. For if we follow God's path, we will travel far beyond even our greatest dreams.